Five Little Penguins Slipping on the Ice

To Mutti, Lopey, Nancy, and Julia

—S.M.

To Andy and Andrea

—L.B.

Library of Congress Cataloging-in-Publication Data

Metzger, Steve.
  Five little penguins slipping on the ice / written by Steve Metzger ; illustrated by Laura Bryant.
      p. cm.
  "Cartwheel Books."
  Summary: A counting book in which one by one the little penguins fall and hurt themselves, to the dismay of their mother and doctor.
   ISBN-13: 978-0-439-77593-9 (pbk.)
   ISBN-10: 0-439-77593-0 (pbk.)
  1. Nursery rhymes. 2. Children's poetry. [1. Nursery rhymes. 2. Penguins--Poetry. 3. Counting.] I. Bryant, Laura J., ill. II. Title.
  PZ8.3.M5596Fhp 2009
  398.8--dc22
  [E]

                                    2008045846

Text copyright © 2002 by Steve Metzger.
Illustrations copyright © 2002 by Laura Bryant.

ISBN-13: 978-0-439-77593-9
ISBN-10: 0-439-77593-0

10 9 8 7 6 5 4   12 13

Printed in the U.S.A.
This edition first printing, September 2009

Five Little Penguins Slipping on the Ice

by Steve Metzger
Illustrated by Laura Bryant

Cartwheel
·B·O·O·K·S·®

SCHOLASTIC INC.
New York   Toronto   London   Auckland   Sydney
Mexico City   New Delhi   Hong Kong   Buenos Aires

Five little penguins slipping on the ice.

One fell down. "Ouch! That's not nice."

The mother called the doctor, and the doctor said,

"No more penguins slipping on the ice!"

Four little penguins sliding near a tree.

One fell into the icy sea!

The mother called the doctor, and the doctor said,

"No more penguins sliding near a tree!"

Three little penguins skating all around.

One flew up and then fell down!

The mother called the doctor, and the doctor said,

"No more penguins skating all around!"

Two little penguins playing on a hill.

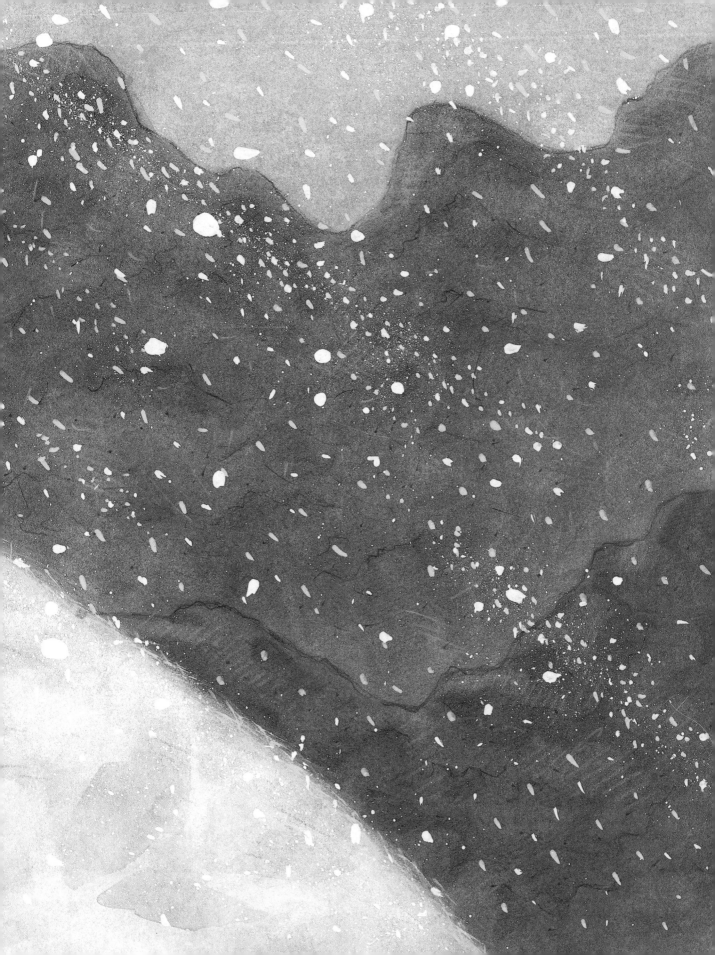

One slipped off and banged her bill.

The mother called the doctor, and the doctor said,

"No more penguins playing on a hill!"

One little penguin jumping very high

Broke the ice and began to cry.

The mother called the doctor, and the doctor said,

"No more penguins jumping very high!"

Now there's…
No little penguins having any fun.
No little penguins, not even one.

The mother called the doctor, and the doctor said,